W9-CBR-398

Holiday House / New York

# Where Crocodiles Have Wings

by Patricia C. McKissack

illustrated by Bob Barner

Printed in the United States of America

The art in this book was created with cut and torn paper from around
the world, as well as paste paper made by the author and his wife.

The text typeface is Avenir Roman.

www.holidayhouse.com

First Edition

1 3 5 7 9 10 8 6 4 2

**Library of Congress Cataloging-in-Publication Data**

McKissack, Pat, 1944–

Where crocodiles have wings / by Patricia C. McKissack;

illustrated by Bob Barner. — 1st ed.

p. cm.

Summary: A rhyming tale describing a magical place where surprises
grow on trees and crocodiles have wings.

ISBN 0-8234-1748-4 (hardcover)

[1. Animals—Fiction. 2. Stories in rhyme.]  I. Barner, Bob, ill. II. Title.

PZ8.3.M224Wh 2005

[E]—dc22

2003067640

ISBN-13: 978-0-8234-1748-3

ISBN-10: 0-8234-1748-4

Designed by Yvette Lenhart

To Mark Fredrick
P. C. M.
To Jean, Joe, and Cathie
B. B.

There's a once-upon-a-place
in time and space
where surprises grow on trees
**And** crocs have wings
Minks wear rings
And chimps are rodeo champs

*If*
You touch your toes
wiggle your nose
**And** slide down an elephant's trunk
Before you can say

Hip Hip **Hooray**

You'll be there just in time
To meet a friend
Around each bend
Who will make you grin and smile
*Like* a young buck deer
Leading a cheer
For the Zebra hockey team

Or if it's spring
hear bullfrogs sing
at the annual nightingale's ball
*Here* bumblebees fish
And peacocks wish
Upon a starry bouquet
*While* hippos prance
And spiders dance
By the light of a square-shaped moon

Just hang with me
And you will see
A wonderful wacky world
**Where**
Turtles go fast
never come last
And win all the races they're in

Coyotes sneeze
And chickens wheeze
Whenever the seasons
change—
**And** bears lay eggs
With two good legs
For running in marathons

It's no surprise
That in disguise
The wolf has taken the cake
**That** camels knit
Socks that will fit
An army of centipedes—
**Or** four-eyed rats
have lunch with bats

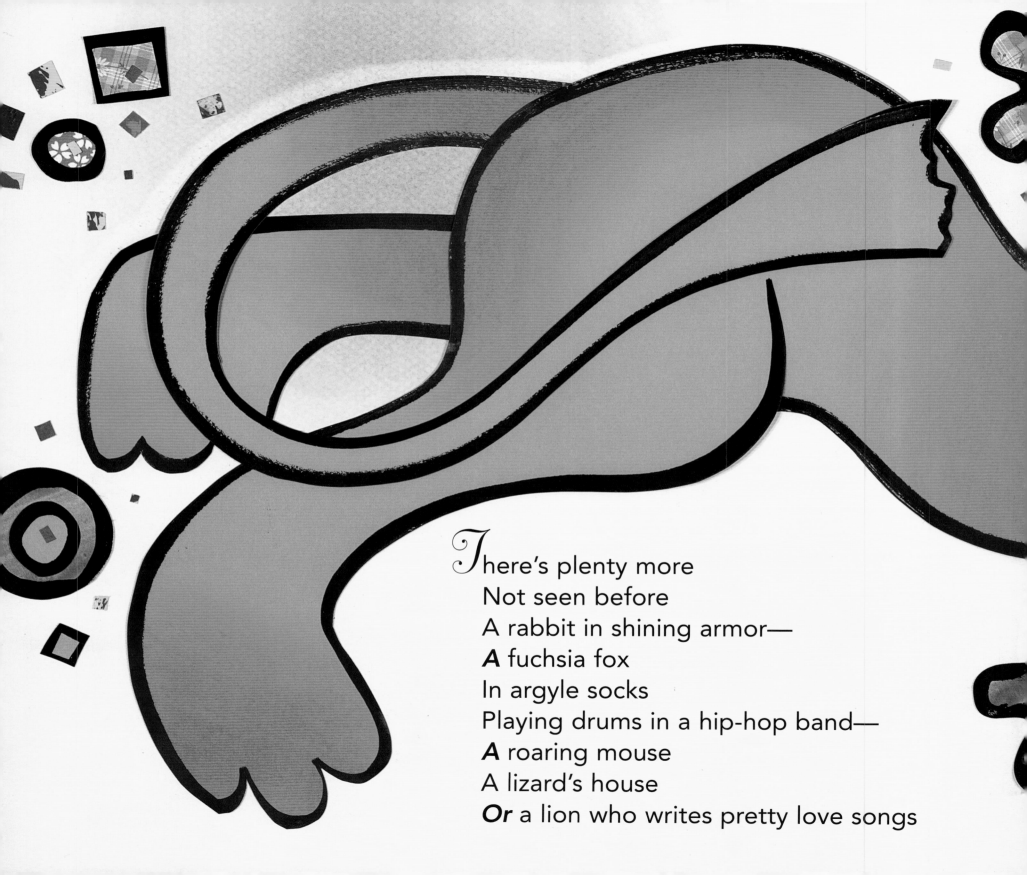

There's plenty more
Not seen before
A rabbit in shining armor—
**A** fuchsia fox
In argyle socks
Playing drums in a hip-hop band—
**A** roaring mouse
A lizard's house
**Or** a lion who writes pretty love songs

Oh, there's never a frown
In this part of town
Even though the end is near

Time to go back
To hit the sack
**So**
**Quick**
Down the elephant's trunk
And before you can say

Hip Hip Hooray

You land in bed at once

*I*'ll show you how
To get there now
Remember what to do
**Touch** your toes
**Wiggle** your nose
and open a favorite book . . .

*A*nd you might see
a fishing bee
*or a crocodile with wings*